RADUAN N

A Cup of Rage

*Translated from the Portuguese
by Stefan Tobler*

A New Directions Paperbook Original

Originally published as *Um copo de cólera* in 1978.

Manufactured in the United States of America
New Directions Books are printed on acid-free paper
First published in 2017 as New Directions Paperbook 1366
Design by Erik Rieselbach

Library of Congress Cataloging-in-Publication Data
Names: Nassar, Raduan, 1935– author. | Tobler, Stefan, translator.
Title: A cup of rage / by Raduan Nassar ; translated by Stefan Tobler.
Other titles: Copo de cólera. English
Description: New York : New Directions Publishing, 2017.
Identifiers: LCCN 2016041669 | ISBN 9780811226585 (acid-free paper)
Classification: LCC PQ9698.24.A838 C613 2017 | DDC 869.3/42—dc23
LC record available at https://lccn.loc.gov/2016041669

10 9 8 7 6 5 4 3 2 1

New Directions Books are published for James Laughlin
by New Directions Publishing Corporation
80 Eighth Avenue, New York 10011

A CUP OF RAGE

*"Nobody guides the one
whom God has led astray"*

*"Hosannah! behold the man!
Narcissus! always remote and fragile,
anarchy's offspring"*

A CUP OF RAGE

The Arrival

AND WHEN THAT afternoon I arrived home at kilometer 27 on the road from town, she was walking around, already waiting for me on the lawn, and came and opened the gate so that I could drive right in, and as soon as I came out of the garage we climbed the stairs together to the conservatory, and no sooner were we there than I opened the middle curtains and we sat down in the wicker chairs, our eyes fixed on the hilltop opposite, where the sun was setting, and the two of us sat in silence until she asked me "what's the matter?" but I, somewhere else entirely, remained distant and still, my thoughts lost in the red sunset, and it was because she repeated the question that I replied "have you eaten yet?" and as she said "later" I got up and wandered over to the kitchen (she followed me), took a tomato from the fridge, went over to the sink and washed it, then went to get the saltshaker from the cupboard and sat down at the table (she followed all my movements from across the room, while I pretended not to notice), and it was under her constant gaze that I began to eat the tomato, sprinkling more salt on what remained in my hand, making a show of biting into it with relish in order to reveal my teeth, strong as a horse's, knowing that she couldn't tear her eyes off my mouth, knowing that beneath her silence she was writhing with impatience, knowing above all that the more indifferent I seemed to be, the more attractive she found me, I only know that when I finished eating the tomato I left her there in the kitchen and went to get the radio that was on the shelf in the living room, and without going back to the kitchen we met again in the hall, and without a word and almost together we entered the half-light of the bedroom.

In Bed

FOR A FEW moments in the room we were like two strangers observed by somebody, and that somebody was always her and me, the two had to watch what I was doing and not what she was doing, so I sat on the edge of the bed and calmly started taking off my shoes and socks, holding my bare feet in my hands and feeling how lovely and moist they were, as if pulled out of the earth that very minute, and then I, with fixed purpose, started to walk around, feigning little reasons for my movements, letting the hems of my trouser-legs brush the floor, at the same time as they partially covered my feet, lending them mystery, knowing that they, bare and very white, powerfully embodied my coming nakedness, and soon I heard her breathing in deeply, over by the chair, where she had perhaps already given in to her desperation, struggling to take off her clothes, getting her fingers caught in the strap slipping down her arm, and I, still faking, knew that all of that was real, oh how I

knew her nightmarish obsession for feet, and for my feet
in particular, their firm step and well-shaped form, a little
bony around the toes perhaps and nervously marked with
veins and tendons on the instep, though they hadn't lost the
shy manner of a tender root, and I went to and fro with my
calculated steps, lengthening the wait more and more with
minimal pretexts, but as soon as she left the room and went
briefly to the bathroom, I quickly took off my trousers and
shirt and throwing myself onto the bed, I waited for her,
stiff and ready, enjoying in silence the cotton of the sheet
that covered me, and right then I closed my eyes thinking
of the stratagems I would use (of all the many I knew), and
in this way I went over alone in my head the things that we
did, how she quivered at the first twitches of my mouth and
at the shine I forged in my eyes, where I brought into plain
view what was most vile and sordid in me, knowing that
carried away by my other side she would always shout "so
this is the bastard I love," and I went over in my head that
other trifling move in our game, a preamble nonetheless to
unexpected later twists and turns, just as necessary a start
as pushing a simple pawn up the board, in which I closed
my hand over hers and straightened out her fingers, instill-
ing courage in them, guiding them under my control to the
hair on my chest, until they, from the example of my fingers
under the sheet, developed their own masterful clandestine
activities, or at a more advanced stage, after having carefully

pored over our hairs, swellings and many smells, when the two of us on our knees measured the longest path for a single kiss, the palms of our hands pressed together, our arms open in an almost Christian exercise, our teeth biting each other's mouths as if biting into the soft flesh of the heart, our eyes closed and our imaginations surrendered to the curves of our circlings, I also saw myself involved in certain practices, such as when, in a trance and already haughtily raised above the saddle of her womb, I would prematurely fulfill one of her (of my) strangest whims, shooting sudden violent jets of milky birdlime which stuck to the skin of her face and the skin of her breasts, or such as that other, less impulsive one, slower to ripen, its fruit developing in a silent and patient crescendo of firm contractions, in which, me inside her, without our moving, with exasperated cries we reached those death rattles of the height of exaltation, and I thought about the dangerous backwards leap, when she on her stomach would generously offer me another pasture, and in which my arms and hands symmetrically and almost mechanically gripped her below the shoulders, pressing and adjusting, part by part, our anointed bodies, and all the time I was thinking of my hands, and the broad backs of them, they were much used in this passionate geometry, so well devised by me, and which invariably led her to say in her perdition "magnificent, magnificent, you're something else," and from there my thoughts drifted

to the restorative moments, the cigarettes we smoked following each poisoned bubble of silence, or during our
conversations over a cup of coffee from the thermos (we
would escape from bed naked and desecrate the kitchen
table), when she would try to describe to me the confused
experience she had when she came, always mentioning my
confidence and boldness as I conducted the ritual, scarcely
hiding her surprise at how I would repeatedly enlist God's
name in my obscenities, telling me above all how much I
had taught her, especially about an awareness of the act
through our eyes that often followed, stone by stone, each
stretch of a convulsing road, and that was when I would
mention her intelligence, which I always praised as the best
thing about her in bed, an agile and active intelligence (even
if only when I pricked her on), exceptionally open to all
incursions, and that would lead to me talking about myself
too, fascinating her with the intentional (some not so intentional) contradictions in my character, teaching her among
other lies that I, the bastard, was pure and chaste, and, there
with my eyes closed all this time, I was still thinking about
many other things while she was out of the room, since
the imagination is very quick, or its time is different, and it
uses and simultaneously confuses separate and unexpected
things, when I discerned her footsteps returning in the hall
and only had time to open my eyes and check that my feet
were positioned correctly, poking out of the bottom of the

sheet, noticing as so many times before that the brown hairs that sprouted on my instep and longer toes gave them both grace and gravitas, but I made sure I quickly closed my eyes again, feeling that she was about to enter the room, and already sensing her fervent form nearby, and knowing how things would start, which is: she would softly, ever so softly, come up to my feet, which she had once compared to two white lilies.

The Rising

IT WAS ALREADY half past five when I said to her "I'm going to jump out of bed" but she wound herself around me like a creeping vine, her claws closing where they could, and she had claws on her hands and claws on her feet, and a thick, strongly smelling birdlime over her whole body, and since we were almost grappling each other I said "let me go, little bindweed," knowing that she liked it when I spoke that way, so in response she said, feigning solemnity, "I won't let you go, my grave *Cypressus erectus*," her eyes beaming with pride at her impressive repartee (although there she wasn't well versed in botanical matters, even less so in the geometry of conifers, and the little that she dared flaunt concerning plants she had learnt from me and nobody else), and in the knowledge that there are no branches or trunks, however strong the tree may be, that can resist the advances of a creeper, I tore myself away from her while there was time and slipped quickly over to the window, immediately raised the blind and felt on my still warm body the cold, damp air that started to get in the room, but even so I leaned on the sill and, deep in thought, saw that outside the day was barely starting to stretch its limbs under the weight of a thick fog, and I also noticed that, no more than sketches, the zinnias in the garden below were struggling to push up through the smudges of smoke, and I was at the window like this, my eyes on the top of the hill opposite, on the spot where the Seminary stood dimly in the fog, when she came up behind me and again wound herself around me, slipping the rope of her arms brazenly around my neck, but with skill I, using my elbows gently, kneading her firm breasts a little, was soon sharing the prison I was in with her, and, side by side, entwined, the two of us gradually interlaced our feet and that was how we went straight to the shower.

The Shower

UNDER THE SHOWER I let her hands slide over my body, and her hands were inexhaustible, and they ran searchingly through all the foam, and they came and went tirelessly, and our soaked bodies now and again pressed against each other so that her hands could reach my back in an embrace, and I enjoyed all this movement, sinuous and vague, that provoked sudden, hidden jolts, and seeing that those hands were already taking advantage of my darkest corners — even combing through the threads at the badly stitched seam of the groin (and secretly weighing the soapy packet of my member) — I said "quick, wash my head, I'm in a hurry," and then, pulling me out from under the stream of water, her hands immediately penetrated my hair, rubbing firmly with her fingers, massaging my scalp with her nails, scratching my nape in a way that sent me crazy, to my core, but I didn't say anything and just carried on feeling the soft foam grow up there until it splashed down onto my face in a rush and stung my eyes, making me rub wildly at them with my knuckles, even though I knew that their burning clearly announced I was clean, and before long she pulled me under the shower again and her fingers in my hair started to tease out the most pleasurable thing in the world under the warm water, and then there was a splat splat as thick foam toppled down, flying apart on the tiles wet with water running noisily into the drain, and she laughed and laughed, and I stood there, so still and abandoned to her care, I didn't raise so much as a finger, so that she would carry out this work on her own, and I was already well rinsed-off when she, straying from the task at hand, slid her wet mouth over my water-skin, but I, taking the reins from her, acted as if nothing had disturbed the ritual, and as soon as she turned the water off I let myself be led silently out of the shower cubicle, and under the light electric current of my shivers I waited there until she threw a large towel over my head, starting immediately to dry my hair with such lithe and precise motions that my memory was jogged, and with my eyes hidden I glimpsed, although small and naked, her feet enlarge in big sandals and I also felt her delicate hands transform themselves suddenly into rustic, heavy hands, though they were minute hands whose fingers entered my ears, heaping caresses on me, tickling me, making me snicker to myself under the towel, and it was so good, her looking after my body and leading me, wrapped up, to the

15

bedroom and combing my hair in front of the mirror and giving me a pretend telling-off and offering me little bits of advice and helping me on with my trousers and shirt and making me lie on my back on the bed, before leaning over me to do up my buttons, and making me place my heavy shoes in her lap so that she, bending over me in her dedication, could tie up my laces, I only know that I delivered myself absolutely into her hands, so that the use she made of my body would be complete.

The Breakfast

WE SMELLED FRESH when we went into the conservatory, where her shoulder bag was still open on the table, and as she sat down in one of the wicker chairs, I opened the curtains still needing to be opened, and half-hidden behind one of the pillars I pressed my nose to the glass and, in spite of the fog, could see Dona Mariana squatting in front of a flower bed down in the garden, her hands in the earth, her watering can at her side, peeping now and then up towards the conservatory's high windows, and that was when I went out onto the landing and, gripping the tiles of the low wall, shouted her name, asking for breakfast, but I immediately entered her field of vision again, her head thrown back on the chair cushion, her skin rosy and relaxed, a short intense sigh as if to say "it wasn't enough, but it will do" (which was what she always told me), and I without a word leaned over the sucupira-wood table, pushed her leather bag and my heavy iron ashtrays aside, and it was at that moment that Dona Mariana came in, acting just like the Protestant mulatto woman she was, patches on her dark and blanched skin, thick-lensed glasses, always greeting us bashfully, but ignoring her embarrassment I immediately ordered "the breakfast," and she knew very well, by my tone, what I wanted to say with this, and knew exactly on which days it had to be served like this in full (my wide bed almost always wide open), so that out of a sense of shame she ran to the kitchen, and in the conservatory I slid the central panes of the French doors to the side, pulled up a chair and sat near the open bit, my eyes hanging on the ill-defined landscape in front of me, and started to contemplate, almost making a real effort, what might be passing through her pure head, and as always I ended up concluding "who cares about your embarrassment, Dona Mariana!, who cares about your lack of understanding, Dona Mariana!, yes, the same wide open bed, but who cares what you think!" and I stirred up the gravel here inside (in reality practising the black art of exorcism), and my maid had already laid the check cloth on the table, and on top of it the crockery, the honey pot, the bowl of fruit, the bread basket and the butter dish, as well as the earthenware jug full of daisies and sensitive fern, and Dona Mariana, still not looking at us, had already gone back, perhaps somewhat calmer now, into the kitchen and in the conservatory we only heard the cheerful clatter of the aluminium pans, and I was thinking how good it was that everything was just like this, when she asked me "what's the matter?" but I, smelling the strong aroma of coffee that was already wafting in great waves from the kitchen, I didn't say anything, didn't even turn my face towards her, but continued to stroke Bingo, my mongrel, and was thinking that the first cigarette of the morning, the one I'd soon be lighting after breakfast, was without the shadow of a doubt one of the seven wonders of the world.

The Explosion

THE SUN ALREADY wanted to do things to the fog, that was easy to see, you only had to look at the cold, porous meat of the mass covering the small farm to realize that a glow as fine as dust was trying to penetrate it, and I remembered that Dona Mariana, her eyes lowered but pleased with her turn of phrase, had said some minutes ago that "yesterday's heat was only a taster," and sitting there in the conservatory I had a good view of what was happening, and my eyes roved over my land's trees and shrubs, not forgetting the smaller things in the garden, and abandoned to this calm pursuit I felt my lungs thank my fingers every time the cigarette rose to my mouth, and she where she sat, I could feel it, was watching me and smoking like me, except that with her there was a tinge of anticipation, certainly questioning me with her spiky gestures, but I wasn't paying that any attention, I wanted silence, since I was enjoying letting my eyes linger on the fresh leaves of the mulberry trees, which stood out in the landscape because of their brazen greenness (beautiful as anything!), but my eyes were suddenly led, and when these things happen you never really know what devil's at work, and, in spite of the mist, I see this: a gap in my hedge, oh misery, I press my finger into the ashtray, get burned, uncomprehending she asked me "what is it?" but without replying I half threw myself, half tripped down the stairs (Bingo was already on the patio, waiting for me, electrified) and she followed me, almost screaming "but what is it?" and Dona Mariana had come running from the kitchen with the commotion, her eyes wide behind her thick lenses, dumbstruck at the top of the stairs, a pot and cloth in her hands, but I didn't see anything, I left the two of them behind and hurtled over, out of my mind, and when I got close I couldn't bear what I saw "fucking leaf-cutter ants," and then I screamed even more loudly "bloody fucking leaf-cutter fucking ants," as I saw whole handbreadths of hedge had been gnawed away, saw whole handbreadths of earth covered with little leaves, you need to have farming blood in your veins to know what this spells, I was rigid as I surveyed the damage, I was livid about that gap, and could only think the privet shouldn't be their feast, such hard work just for the leaf-cutters to set their maws to it, and in a flash I rushed, armed, to the neighboring plot, and straight away found the trail that would lead me to their colony, following the path concealed in the high grass, I who at this hour would surprise them in their hideaway—those who'd been so active all night with the cutting and harvesting, and without delay, trembling and foaming, I find it and already holding the bucket in my hand I pour a double dose of poison into each anthill, with a malice that only I know for what it is because only I know what I feel, livid with these wonderfully orderly ants, livid with their model efficiency, livid with how fucking organized they are that they left the weeds well alone and ate my privet hedge, for that I apportioned them one hell of a binge, flooding their tunnels with a thick broth of insecticide, careful not to leave anything there alive by grinding closed the mouths of the tunnels with my heel, and I was already coming back from that barren plot, sending sparks flying as I went, when I noticed that she and Dona Mariana by this point were having a chat on the patio between the house and the lawn, her little bum leaned against the car's mudguard, the brightness of the day quickly restoring her confidence as an emancipated chit, her dress of a carefully chosen simplicity, her bag hung from one shoulder down to the opposite hip, a cigarette between her fingers, and prattling away ever so democratically with a common person, that being one of her favorite accessories by the way, she, of all people, who never deigned to visit the house's utility room, having me serve her in bed and the housekeeper serve her in the conservatory, leaving breakfast to me if Dona Mariana wasn't around, I only know that, with an irritated look on my face, and without a glance at them, I stooped and entered the tool cupboard under the stairs, left the equipment there that I had taken to finish off the leaf-cutters, but thinking ahead I used the supplies on the shelves to stock up with other poisons, as well as swigging away surreptitiously in that rustic chamber, among the brushes, charcoal and leftover paint, at a gallon of acid, concerned as I was to redecorate my guts, knowing in advance that it wouldn't be in vain, I only know that when I went out to the patio again the two weren't talking any more, and although side by side, were very wisely standing apart, not only had she made the housekeeper her audience, but she was waiting for me with this look, just unbelievable, that made me want to give her a slap, and as if that weren't enough she also said, "it's not a big deal, especially for a rational little boy like you," and I have to admit that "little boy" was a kick in the shins, that was tough, even more so because of how she said it, for it contained that poised casualness she put in everything, which in this case was a sort of distancing, as though distance alone could necessarily lend the comment its reasonableness, and this only served to make me even more angry, "right" I said to myself as if I were saying "now's the time," and I getting hung up on that "boy" could perfectly well have said to her, "time has taken more of a toll on me" (although she wouldn't have understood what advantage I drew from this), and could also have given her an earful for her essentially boring use of a nasty irony, not that I nurture a boiling hunger for harsh words, a bent towards the tragic, it was neither that nor the opposite, but it would do her good, she who saw in her irony the exercise of high intelligence, if I were to sensibly remind her that irony and a solid character don't mix, and I could have said many other things in reply to her comment, because it was easy to see, half-revealed, half-hidden, multiple accusations in her words, whether of my extreme dedication to animals and plants, or the perhaps even stronger accusation that I didn't act at that same temperature in bed (that is, with the same ardor that I had in exterminating the ants), and what's more she, her eye on the blood of the thermometer, had also made it her job to regulate reasoning's mercury, not suspecting that my reason was at that moment working at full steam, suspecting even less that reason is never cold and passionless, the contrary only believed by those who don't in their reflections reach the powering core, to see this you need to be penetratingly sharp, not that she wasn't intelligent, without a doubt she was, but not enough, just what would do, and I could daringly have given my reasoning free rein, squeezing to a pulp the kernel of her sarcasm, but I didn't say a thing, not a squeak, I locked my word away, she didn't have enough, just what would do, I was thinking, that was why she was already oiling her viper's tongue, which had been numb all night, snuggled up against

my feet and etcetera, I only know that I continued to advance with my head down, the things here inside grinding
away, and Dona Mariana, this was easy to see, was first in
line, but it wasn't Dona Mariana, nor was it her, it wasn't
anyone in particular to make things perfectly clear, but even
so I asked "where's Antônio?" and I asked the housekeeper
this in a more or less calm way and like someone who almost, but only almost, has himself under control, but nor
did it matter if it wasn't like that, my stomach itself was a
nest of ants and they were coming up my throat, not to
mention that I was already pulling onto the stage whoever
was within reach, for it wasn't going to be to her liking, but,
sui generis, I was to put on a show without an audience,
that's why I challenged the once again bashful Dona Mariana harshly, asking her "where's Antônio?" this time making
my voice as mean as the mask of my face, using both tools
together, the pliers and the crowbar, to wrench a word out
of her, not that I was about to demand that her husband
compensate me for the gap, not that he could be made responsible for the ants' fury, but—harnessed to my rage—
like a horse, I only needed a starting shot, a reply, only a
reply, any throw-away phrase from the housekeeper would
be enough "Tônio's just gone down there, but he'll be right
back," or more cautiously Dona Mariana could justify his
absence "he left very early to get the milk at the store and
must be almost back by now," or she could even, in one of

her bursts of eloquence, say drily, "Tônio was in one of the anthills and must be in his last convulsions now along with the leaf-cutters," and even were she to say, with some truth as it happens, that it wouldn't have made a difference whether her husband was there or not, explaining to me (as if it were news) that leaf-cutters tended to work in the black of night, the truth was it didn't matter what she told me, only an idiot wouldn't have seen that, and whether her reply was conscientious or aloof, I only know that no sooner had Dona Mariana opened her mouth than I came charging out: "I've already told you that the hours here are six to four, after that I don't even want to see you in the house, nor to stumble across him, but within these hours I won't allow it, do you understand? and you should tell that to your husband, are you listening?" and my roar was strong, even if its only substance was its vibration (which isn't to be scoffed at), and its effect was such that Dona Mariana didn't know what to do, whether to call her husband so that he could do what I had just ordered (apart from the fact that I had only demanded he take care, it was perfectly well known that his hours started at seven, not six), or to go upstairs to the kitchen, or even whether she should stay to open the gate for the little miss, who in a provisional rebuke had just grasped her door handle, and the best that Dona Mariana rummaged out of her head, after much excited flapping about, was to stand a little to the side, wisely hidden by the corner of the house and near to the stairs, but she didn't climb them or do anything else, and that was when she, still holding the handle, swallowing the perfect kernel of my bait, and putting on, as befitted the situation, the air of someone who discusses serious matters (she could act this role well), came on stage again of her own accord, and said to me fairly calmly, "I don't understand how this change comes over you, suddenly you turn into a fascist" and she said this in a more or less serious tone, a straight objective commentary, only adding a little more of a twist to the corners of her mouth, so that her expression ended up sketching how repulsive the thing was, and that got me in the balls, and it wasn't my balls that deserved to get it, I was sure (in spite of everything), was sure that my rage would be washed clean in its fount, "you perplex me" she added in the same serious tone, "perplex me!," but I held steady, didn't move for a while except to pick up two or three logs from the ground, feeding dry wood to the fire that I was just starting (I who was—methodically—mixing reason and emotion into an exquisite alchemical amalgam), after all she still hadn't got into her car, I knew her, she wasn't the type to say something and then get in, on the contrary she was one of those women who only needle you in the greedy expectation of receiving a good beating, so much so that when she pricked me she already had her eye on the satisfying wood for my fire, in any case she had really got to me, or was I rather, an actor, only faking, to follow an example, the pain that I really felt,* I who this time had gone right into myself and in the heat here inside knew what changes I was capable of (I wasn't a monolithic block, no one is of course, and then there's the fact that certain traits she attributed to my personality had more to do with the situation), but I wasn't going to mention this to her, yes, I could take up her challenge and launch myself into a battle royal, comfortingly with shared content, knowing that in spite of her impatience she wouldn't scorn a good preamble, I only had to pretend that I was falling into the trap, nibbling all the while at the bait, sucking at the kernel of sweet corn as if sucking the nipple of her breast, while to pick a fight it was enough to hurl the classic words "you're hardly the one to teach me how to treat a maid," remembering straight after that nothing stops whoever's stepping on someone else from protesting about the person stepping on them, but that you always need to start by looking at your own paws, your body before clothes, this heartfelt revelation that precedes communion, and, if I had wanted, I could've found plenty of reasons to trip her up, not that I was so naïf I demanded coherence, I didn't expect that of her, I didn't even boast of that myself, only idiots and bastards proclaim that they serve a single lord, in the end we are all beasts born of one and the same

---

* Translator's notes begin on page 67.

dirty womb, carriers of the most vile contradictions, but if someone were to flaunt their morals, then right from the start that person should admit to a complete lack of shame, the truth being that all these quarrels among the hand-wringing children of the petite bourgeoisie really got my goat, as they guilelessly vied for the most generously soft boots, even extracting from their comparisons an air of liberal virtue, and how she loved this purgative, just as she would purge herself by giving the middle class a good whipping, this class that is almost always hated, perhaps for this reason vacillating between soaring to the heights of the eagle or trudging the earth in humble sandals, sometimes so indecisive as to confuse the direction of those two poles, was it an ascent towards priesthood or a dive on prey? (and how not to arrive there, gloriously?), but it didn't even enter my head to goad the fraud where she was most conflicted, I wasn't going to confuse a fine needle with the immanently bruising power of my bludgeon, other motives would be needed to put me on a war footing, I was far from being interested in the common traits of a banal character, and nor was I going to pull on her hook and so encourage the usual veering of her reasoning, not that the claws she put in her words scared me, I too, besides my gentle face (with perhaps the odd sly look), knew how to give words their reverse, the grimaces and talons, incisive like her I knew the best way to bite with the teeth of ideas, since our intrigues tended to be made of these shards, not to mention that my hoofs—driven along a strict lane—knew how to invent their own logic, but all this discursive aggression was verging exhaustively on the monotonous, it was no longer about yawning over an uneasy night's sleep, it wasn't that annoying habit of stretching out your arms unnecessarily, in my fever the things here inside were rapidly melting together, I didn't have any sand in my gizzard, let alone the gravel that was more suitable to digesting her talk, not forgetting that reflection is nothing more than the excretions of the drama of our existence, foolishly put on a pedestal by us, but as Antônio had already fertilized the vegetable beds the week before, what were we to do with this theoretical chaff? so, quick as lightning I found a way out, off on a tangent, and where I went was land she had staked out and fenced in, an area where she prided herself on being a free little bird, that was where I'd get her, only there would I open a gap in her defences (I who could simply dismiss her with a summary "get lost," turn my back on her and go up to the conservatory), it was there that I'd exasperate her arrogant rationality, but nor was that what I wanted (to simply exasperate her), I was inside myself, in that instant I needed a prop, needed more than ever—in order to act—the screams of a supporting actress, and let me be perfectly clear: I didn't want the bleatings of an audience, far from it, I was fully aware that I only wanted to get back my lost shriek, and she didn't even have much to do with all this (yes, it's confusing, but that's how it was), I was inside myself, as I just said (chaos!), I was dealing with an imbroglio, with the colic, with terrible contortions brought on by this flush, with things that fermented in the tunnel of my stomach, all the things that existed outside and that my ants had carried, bit by bit, and were they ever great at carrying, the fuckers, plain excellent at it, and the damned insects had found every possible entrance into me, my eyes, my nostrils, my ears, especially my earholes! and someone had to pay, someone always has to pay, whether they wanted to or not, that was one of life's axioms, that was a natural prop for rage (and sometimes even the best relief from guilt), the fact is that even feeling eyes on me—Dona Mariana's Protestant eyes were ready, and I had already found Antônio's shaky legs behind a bush—even so I stuck my chest out a little and took two steps towards her, and she must have noticed some solemnity in how I approached her, she was an intelligent little miss, and fickle, the bitch, I only know that she suddenly put her hands on her waist, her face became two defiant eyes, the two ends of her mouth turned sarcastic, and she squandered other gaudy little gestures, most of them completely unnecessary, at this point I could no longer contain a violent "hey you, you," I suddenly let fly "you, you shitty little journalist," I continued expelling my bile in bursts, she stood quite still by the car, only her little bum rubbed against the door handle, and the bitch smiled, laughed a "ha ha hah" that I had and hadn't expected, she was trying to confuse me, but even so I continued to advance, "why insist on trying to teach me, you shitty little journalist? why insist on trying to teach me when the little that you learnt in life you learnt from me, from me" and I hammered on my chest and was already raising my voice to a shout, but she said "oh! honorable master! ..." and with a swish-whoosh her venomous tongue came out and back, unbelievable how that well-oiled instrument worked, and hearing what she said I shook, not exactly because of her irony, which didn't go beyond an amateurish attempt to defend herself, rather it was her obsession with castrating me, calling me "master" yes, yet as always denying my access to knowledge because of my lack of titles, I was the "graduate odd-job man" (what did the fraud know of my work and my affairs?), suggesting that I stick to my usual territory in our discussions, although I couldn't care less by then, I mean, I wasn't interested in being venerated in the field of ideas, and anyway I had said to her many times that the quality of someone's thought wasn't seen in their profession, nor in their head, but in their throat, in the stubborn girth of the gullet when they swallow, an anatomical defect that is just as rare among common mortals as it is among stupid intellectuals, and so it's from a sickness—and only from there—that the bitter force of independent

thought comes, obviously the prophets can't be held responsible for the sensuality of their followers, but I used to
go rigid when I saw the fraud, anointed with the spirit of the
times, surrendering herself lasciviously to the myths of the
moment, I used to go rigid when I saw the fraud, in spite of
her affected rebelliousness, being pulled here or there by
this or that owner, I tried many fucking times to slip a pen-
knife in under her dog collar, many fucking times I said to
her that every chained dog hides a wild one, to her, who at
every opportunity would refer me to her guides (she was as
strong as iron, the fraud, it was impossible to harm her bone
structure), despairingly I'd tell her that rather than esoteric
ghouls it was I who held my existence in my hands, not
knowing, apart from the womb, a mold capable of giving
this raw material form, but it was always heresy to touch her
idols' tablets of the law, to draw a line in the dust, to scare
off the ghosts, I even reminded her of the episode with that
wanderer from earlier times (were he around now, she
would be his spaniel, join his school, lick his feet in an obscene display of submission), who in his natural history
incorrectly attributed a certain number of teeth to the
horse, and whose slow but authoritative pace meant that his
mistake passed down the centuries as if it were true, and
also of many other absurdities, some there since primordial
times, that continued to be idiotically carried on high litters, and that even in schools (the altars of dogma) people

formed lines to let such litters pass, but it didn't do any good to preach against them, it didn't do any good to turn the key to unlock the door, I "an odd-job man" (a graduate in odd jobs), I was not a "master," much less "honorable," I (the irony) was certainly not an authority and yet even so I had the sudden urge—and this wasn't the first time—to put two fingers at each end of my lips, stretching them until the mouth of my forge was wide open, and at the same time winking in a clear admonition to "open my mouth and count this horse's teeth for yourself," thus giving a grotesque illustration of the force of empiricism, since I was no more to her than a "vaguely interesting animal," this by the way, in her unconvulsive hours, was the most she granted me, but I didn't say or do any of all that, I didn't bare my teeth, or do anything comparable, the effort wouldn't exactly be educational after all, and as I've already said, I didn't want the bleatings of an audience, and as I've also already said, I wanted to get back my lost shriek, I only haven't yet said— and this is the most important thing—that I wanted to stick to my usual territory, and so I tackled her viciously "it never occurred to you, did it? you shitty intellectual, it never oc- curred to you that everything you say and everything you vomit up is all stuff that you've heard from other people, that you haven't done any of the stuff you talk about, that you only screwed like a virgin and that without my crowbar you aren't any-fucking-thing, that I've got a different life and a different weight," but there she interrupted me "go on, go on, say it once more, tell me that you aren't the great hermit I imagine you to be, but that you have a ton of demons around you, go on, say it, say it again … ha ha hah … you demon … ha ha hah …" she must have scoffed a whole tub of brilliantine for breakfast, I'd never said anything like that! it was clear that things were slipping out of control, I for my part was shaking, and so was on the way to losing it, to loosening my tongue much more than was acceptable "listen here, fraud, don't talk about what you don't understand, mouth off in your press, go and preach your sermons there, denounce repression, teach what is just and what is unjust, go and pour your drop on the torrent of words; waste the paper of your newspaper, but don't poke your maw into the leaves of my privet" I said, angry as hell with myself for suddenly being simply on the defensive after my sharp and crude attack, allowing crafty her to stab me with absolute precision "quite understood, sir, I'm more than capable of gauging your fears … such modesty, such a need for security, all this oh-so-suspicious concern for your hedge, and by the way it's unbelievable how you are mirrorizing yourself in what you say; go on, talk, don't stop all those words, don't stop your portrait, but afterwards come and see your face from here … ha ha hah … disgusting!" and she said it as if she were catching me in the act, and took advantage of my confusion to twist the blade in further "build a wall, a fort, protect what you own behind a thick wall" "don't draw easy conclusions" I managed to squeeze in, "it's what the people conclude" she retorted, making it clear that the only thing left to do was pronounce sentence, probably the medieval wheel, "do you know who you remind me of, do you, you fraud?" I said in a level voice, unable to believe in the sudden calm of each word (all of them still nervous inside), pretending you see that I was going to get into the battle royal, use her methods (she insisted on the preamble, wanted, before the beating, for me to light up the buttons of her body), but I rode off on my own calculations, simmering away under the pot's lid you could see my numbers jiggling around in the bubbles "you remind me of a man who dresses as a woman for carnival: he straps on enormous conches of rubber as breasts, paints two scarlet circles on his cheeks and heavy eyeliner over his lashes, pads out his buttocks with cushions, and then he's off, with enough swing in his hips to make even the most flexible dark girl envious; his figure is so striking that the guy manages — although the hair on his arms and legs betrays him — to be more of a woman than a real woman" "and? ..." "and that makes me think about how dogmatism, caricatures and depravity often go together, and that privileged people like you, dressed up as *the people*, generally look to me like carnival trannies," and what I said was absolutely clear, without any interruption that might disturb my illustration, but her agility was amazing, it wasn't only in her use of populism, in her style too she achieved a transcendent mimicry "every citizen has the right to paint two scarlet circles on their cheeks, why not!, decorate their nose with a red ball, hang a thick, crooked stick from their arm as a walking stick, put on a pointy hat, and, once they've done that, go and joke around on the main square ... ha ha hah ... ha ha hah ... ha ha hah ..." I ought to have congratulated the fraud, I didn't have her talent, my cynicism didn't go that far, to put on a show of indifference so close to a bonfire, to guffaw with laughter just before the sacrifice, I had to acknowledge her skill at imitation, my head was a little blank for a moment, I felt my legs had suddenly been amputated, I fell into a total paralysis, and noticed out of the corner of my right eye Dona Mariana—peering round the corner of the house—quickly pull her head back, and out of the corner of my left eye I could clearly see—stuck between the bush's branches—Antônio's slow face, oh, she was enjoying having an audience all right "take it easy, fraud, people like you fulfill a function" I said bitterly, "take it easy, know-it-all, people like you fulfill a function too— with your arms crossed you'd just be a conniver, but now I see that's not enough, you'll be judged as a perpetrator!" "I didn't ask your opinion" I said, leaning on this set phrase, a

lazy cliché but, to compensate, one able to stir up what remained of my muscles, I felt that two gigantic balls were
bursting here on my biceps as I reconquered—highest ad-
venture!—my conscience that had been occupied, thus
sickness and sovereignty came together of necessity "to
judge what I say and what I do I have my own courts, I don't
delegate it to third parties, I don't recognize in anyone—in
absolutely anyone—the moral power to weigh my actions"
I said, with a sudden change in rhetoric (I had struck the
tuning fork and picked up a suspect tone, but simple instru-
ments that they were—even the unutterable ones—how
could words be guilty, considering that everything depends
on context? what we had were useless solutions), and re-
versing the proportions once and for all, tossing in three
shovelfuls of cement to each one of sand, mixing a different
bond into the discourse, and reserving for myself a chaste
communion wafer and a superb goblet of wine I began
firmly and cohesively (as well as masterfully, like an actor)
to intone the liturgy of a black mass "I was thirteen when I
lost my father, never did I don mourning clothes, nor did I
even then suffer any feeling of abandonment, and so I'm not
looking for a new father-son bond now, my history would
have to be remade for me to give up being an orphan" "con-
gratulations on that fine deed" she said casually "only you
manage to be an orphan and an old man at the same time
… ha ha hah …" and as well as diverting the course of what

I had said, her sarcasm forged a subtle addition: a suggestion that her lumping me in the gray generation would an-
noy the hell out of me, I of all people, I, who even cultivated
old age prematurely, and the fraud knew it, she wasn't un-
aware of what she herself called my "superfluous preten-
sion," which only set off the daring contortionism of her
reply all the more, even more so bearing in mind that I had
some white hairs, which had been appearing chronologi-
cally, by force of time, but that I was far from having salt-
and-pepper hair (the twists and turns of her logic were
brilliant, without a doubt she deserved to be complimented
on them), in truth, brilliance aside, her mockery hid as always a fog of sensuality, the same plaintive, provocative and
redundant appeal, in short the little miss could never get
enough of this "old man," I only know that I continued in
the saddle of my calculations, although, while in full control, I must admit that she was still tugging on my numbers'
ear, for in spite of the time being up that I had allowed myself for the battle royal, I saw myself quickly binding—tying
one end to another—the thread she had just cut "I said and
I repeat: my history would have to be remade for me to give
up being an orphan, I know that's impossible, but that
would be the very first condition; the time has gone when
I saw living together as viable, only demanding, piously, my
share of the common good, the time has gone when I con-
sented to a contract, leaving out many things, although not
what was most vital to me, the time has gone when I recog-

nized the shocking existence of imagined values, the spine of all "order"; but I didn't even have the air I needed to breathe, and with that denied me, I was suffocating; being conscious of this frees me, it drives me on, I dwell on other things, today the universe of my problems is different; in a world without rhyme or reason—definitely out of focus—sooner or later everything gets reduced to a point of view, and you, spending all your time cooing over the humanities don't even realize that you're cooing over a joke: it's impossible to tidy up the world of values, you can't clean the devil's house; so I refuse to think about what I don't believe in any more, whether that be love, friendship, the family, the church, humanity; I couldn't care less about all that! my existence still terrifies me, but I'm not afraid of being alone, exile was a conscious choice, I'm satisfied with the cynicism of those great people who are indifferent towards everything ..." "oh, he's metaphysicalizing now, is Mr. Speculation ... if I slacken the reins he immediately shoots off into asinine twaddle ... don't come with that, you're out-of-date" she said brusquely, dismissing any criticism, sealing my protests, filing them away without consultation, slipping a solid iron ring over my bundle of ideas, perhaps there was something of the bull about me (my long, languid eyelashes?), but you also have to admit that in committing such violence to my horse's nostrils she went too far, while insisting on her own frivolous rights, taking a delicious pleasure in stretching the elastic words, chewing on this one or that

as if it were a rubber band or her dad's dick, "mirrorizing,"
the dirty bitch, "metaphysicalizing" in her special way, I
needed to call a halt to this whole farce, it had already gone
on far too long as a preamble, I'd groped her bait too long,
the fraud, I had a feeling that the moment was approaching
when her hook would tear my mouth "you're impossible,
Ms. Bureaucrat, but I'm not going to resist this statement,
it's important: it was with great effort that I learnt to wear
my stigma elegantly, now I feel my hands are powerful and
free, can do things, obviously with one eye on the policeman on the corner, and one eye on clandestine orgies; this
is the enlightenment that can be revealed to excluded people, along with the will to use a spark of that light to set fire
to the pages of any rule book," and that was when she had a
brainwave, "I've had" she said, adding in English, "*an insight*," as if she were having a eureka moment, "I think I've
worked out the puzzle, I've finally discovered what our odd-
job man's real "occupation" is, what I'm saying is, it's only
now that I finally understand why you were so loath to
speak about your "work," why so much "mystery," only now
do I understand your affairs, now that all the clues lead me
to deduce that you are no more than a no-good con man, a
rat, a forger" before adding a final snub "you're not any old
forger, you're a graduate forger..." and I have to confess that
my legs started to shake again, in that precise moment I saw
Bingo cut an electric line through the space between her

and me, his shiny black fur stringing another wire in the air, and in his wake I stretched the cord of my nerves even further, carefully avoiding the suspicion of being a forger, which by the way I didn't know whether it was said in jest or not, or if, being the one, the other wasn't prudently part of the mix, I only know that I passed over it, I refrained from discussing the merits of what she said, didn't permit her to gauge the seriousness of her supposed discovery, left the fraud clutching at nothing as, with a magician's sleight-of-hand, I made the apple of her *insight* vanish "today I feel relieved of obligations, of course I would have preferred the weight of duties to that of freedom; I didn't have a choice, I was chosen, and if on the one hand my destiny was revealed to me, on the other hand destiny took it on itself to reveal me: I'm responsible for absolutely nothing, I'm no longer master of my own steps, the path I walk is the broad one, all I do, I already said, is to keep one eye on the policeman on the corner, the other on clandestine orgies" "oops, better pay attention, else he'll send his words into orbit again … cut the pomposity and descend from your heights, learn O Stratospheric One that going up is easy, the real trick is how you come down afterwards; so don't come with talk of your destiny, fate, karma, scar, mark, branding, stigma, all this paraphernalia that you bizarrely christen as your "history"; if our metaphysician here would put his feet on the ground, he would see that this messed-up world only needs rational

solutions, it doesn't much matter that they have their limits,
what matters is that they are the best ones at the time; only
an idiot would refuse controls on something so precarious,
and don't forget that in life's rough-and-tumble motives
aren't the point—although this little question seems to be
doing your head in—it's all about moving the ball forward,
history is pushed onwards by the friendly hand of assassins
too; the heights you aspire to, by the way, your perfectionist
fancies, they had to lead to this: the authoritarian drivel of
a scummy iconoclast—the old elephant in the china shop,
and to top it all, you talk in those tragic tones, like the pro-
totype of some class in its last agony ... get lost, carcass!"
and she immediately wrote my performance off as cathartic
("pure catharsis" she mumbled), a terrifyingly destructive
word and which—through its imprudent use, its abuse—
transformed the fraud's very brain into an atomic mush-
room cloud, but again I passed over it, even leaving the
"paraphernalia" behind (move the ball forward!) and was
pushing my own history onwards, working out a tropical
algebra, as heated as its origins (blood and sand), a perfect
operation that didn't dispense with the fraud's positive values nor give up my negative values (or the "friendly hand of
assassins"): "I already said that the margins of society used
to torment me, the margins are now a saving grace, I was
repelled when I wanted to take part, let the world go to the
dogs now! let cities fall, let people suffer, let life and free-

dom perish, when the ivory king's under threat, who cares about the flesh and blood of sisters and mothers and children? the soul isn't heavy though sons are dying in the distance,"* "ha ha hah … he's lost it … ha ha hah … you crook!" "everything can come tumbling down, I'll turn my back on it; meet absurdity with madness, and there could be no other response—yes, it's a bitter one, but at least it's appropriate, and it doesn't depend on what you decree, because it's easy to see now what your future holds: as well as meeting all the requirements to be an excellent journalist, you are perfectly suited for the women's police; oh, and one more thing, as an abuse of power I can't see any difference between an editor-in-chief and a chief of police, just as there's no difference between a newspaper boss and a government boss, and both are in cahoots with other kinds of bosses" "it's not me you'll have to deal with one day, you pompous crook, but the people" "just once, you fraud, look at what's staring you in the face, even if it is at odds with your folklore, even if your ears aren't made for such dissonant tones: the people will never take power!" "village idiot! … he's really having convulsions now, who knows what else will come of this fit …" "the people will never take power! so it won't be them I have to deal with one day; hurt and humiliated, the people are only, and always will be, a ruled mass that, by the way, says stupid things which you exalt, without realizing that in general the people say and think what the powers-that-be allow; they actually speak for themselves when they speak (as I do) with the body, which doesn't help much, because their identity never blends with their supposed representatives' identity, and because the shitty strong arm of authority is necessarily the basis of all "order," a rather shrewd word, as it happens, that simultaneously incorporates an unbearably commanding voice and a presumption of where things should be; of course the people can reap some benefits, but always only as the mass that emerging leaders manipulate; so, forward, fraud, forward—with the people in your mouth, parroting their simple if picturesque speech, stuffing your mimicry down the throats of the already suffocating sheep, just like the impassive ventriloquist who puts the little ones on his knee like a good father, and even uses his art to reveal some tricks, while still tricking them by concealing his own voice; but don't worry, fraud, you'll get there ... riding, naturally, your usurped revolt, riding your second-hand revolt; but as for this crook, this lost son here, I've just got one thing to say: nobody guides the one whom God has led astray! which is why I accept neither this pigsty we've got nor any other "order" that might be established, so listen—" I said reaching the zenith of my liturgy and, thinking of the supposed ascent of my words, I lowered my tone dirtily to compensate: "I've got balls, fraud, I don't need a higher power!" "hosannah! behold the man! Narcissus! always remote and fragile, anarchy's offspring! . . . ha ha hah! . . . he's dogmatic, a caricature and depraved . . . ha ha hah!" "get this, fraud, all "order" privileges some people and things" "get this, you crook, disorder does too — it privileges brute force, for starters" "plain brute force, without any legitimizing law" "I'm talking of the law of the jungle" "which doesn't put on a show of modesty, doesn't allow space for hypocrisy, and doesn't unjustly call on aseptic reason as a crutch" "so put on a loincloth, or do without one, gorilla-boy" "I'll do without your advice, you stay there, in your circle of light, and leave me here, in my thick darkness, I didn't start wallowing in this blackness yesterday; I haven't cultivated a seraphic paleness, I don't lend my eyes a pious look, nor do I ever put a saintly mask on my face, nor nourish the hope of seeing my image enthroned on an altar; unlike good Samaritans I don't love my neighbor, nor know who that would be, to be short about my preferences: I don't like people; after all, fraud, someone has to — and now I'll use your magic little word — 'assume' the role of the story's shadowy villain, someone has to assume it at the very least so you can keep your bright halo hovering above the back of your head; so I'll take on all evil, since the divine is as much in evil as it is in holiness; and then, fraud, if I can't be loved, I'll be most content to be hated" "with reason out of reach, he now ridiculously resuscitates himself as Lucifer . . . ha ha hah . . . sound and fury . . . ha ha hah . . . you're nothing

more than a by-product of hidden passions, and all this
mumbo jumbo that you go into such detail about, only
serves, by the way, to confirm some old suspicions of mine
… between ourselves, a moral aberration is always the offspring of unconfessable aberrations, only that can explain
your 'whims' … along with, of course, why an active woman
like me scares you … and as for your arrogant, contempla-
tive 'exile,' it's clear as day now: banished by the collective
consciousness that never tolerates weaklings, you had to
live out in the country; in our ecologist's favor, however, it
will be remembered that he didn't wheel in pollution as his
reason for leaving, thus imitating those master swindlers
who—to better hide their real motives—let fools grasp
their own despicable conclusions from what looks obvious,
a perfect game to play as it happens: it leaves everyone
happy—while the first, playful lot enjoys its trick in silence,
the other, noisy lot celebrates its shrewd judgment; but
that's not the case with you: a swindler but not a master,
what should have stayed hidden ended up obvious too, it
backfired, as this was your only possible 'destiny': to live in
a hideaway with someone of your kind … Lucifer and his
rabid dog … that could be turned into a film … ha ha hah
… one of the them closing the little gaps in the hedge, the
other standing guard until night arrives, both of them doing
their utmost to secure their private sphere, and then afterwards, on the quiet … mutually … between scratching and

licking ... elaborating with their little muzzles their clandestine orgies ... ha ha hah ... ha ha hah ... ha ha hah ... it makes me sick!" her words hailed down on me, picking up more with a steady hand, she flung reason in my face again and stabbed me with sharp spines, I held back my slobber, but my teeth were clacking, for that reason alone I started punching holes in the hemorrhagic discourse of my cerebral stroke, "yes, me, who's been led astray, yes, me, the enraged individualist, me, the enemy of the people, me, the irrationalist, corrupted me, with my epilepsy, delirium and madness, passionate me ..." "burn me, O Fiery Mouth! ... ha ha hah ..." " ... me, the convulsing wick, me, the spark of confusion, me, inflamed matter, me, perpetual heat, me, the destroying flame ..." "transform me into your glowing embers! ... ha ha hah ..." "me, the experienced handler of my trident, me, who cooks up a giant pot of sulfur, me, always licking my lips at children's sweet flesh ..." "oh sweet and violent fire! ... ha ha hah ..." "me, the cyst, the sore, the canker, the ulcer, the tumor, the wound, the body's cancer, me, all this without any irony and much more, but I don't hide my own appetites behind the hunger of the people; and know this too, that I don't give a shit for all your blather, and it's only my good hygiene that keeps me from wiping my ass on your humanism; I already said I have a different life, a different weight, you dwarf of a woman, you just can't get that into your head" I said, pouring my bile into the

blood of my words, feeling I'd knocked a bone or two of
hers awry, I'd hit home about the disguise, not to speak of
the preemptive rejection of her humanism, but her agility
was just amazing, seeing that there wasn't room for more
words in this fight the dwarf, although she was annoyed,
quickly grabbed the tail end of my rocket and simultaneously—with an eloquent cock of her hips—started inciting
me to fight, saying "a little boy, magnificent in all he does . . .
you old fascist!," she pronounced her sentence in two
clearly distinct tones, and where the first implied a forced
mockery, with a feral bit of evil curled round it, the second
implied a final seriousness, with a wisp of hurt coiled round
it, and so I, although shaking, started to advance more con-
fidently, and get my breath back without her noticing, and
since I was recovering the calm of each word (all of them
still nervous inside), I risked saying "just one question: do
you know what I think of you, compared to me?" "you are
incapable, absolutely incapable of having an opinion" "all
right, but do you know what I think of you and of me, com-
paring us?" "spit it out, you little crook" "I admit that in
certain moments I turn into a fascist, I do and I know I do,
but you turn into one too, just like me, it's just that when
you do, you don't know it; that's the only difference between us, just that;* and you only don't know that you've
turned into one because—although this is hardly new—
nothing is more fashionable today than to be a fascist in the

name of reason" "so can I conclude that our fascist who's confessed is actually better, compared to me" "not at all, if on the one hand it's a saving grace, on the other hand confession can also liberate me: to be more of a fascist than ever …" "what are you trying to say?" and her eyes pecked at me, challenged me, "are you threatening me?" but from the corner of my eye I noticed that Bingo was stiffening his body to a statue, his eyes boring into her, his tail straight as a length of wood, his ears two antennae, a mongrel yes, but in the poised position of a dog that's found its prey, "keep out of it, Bingo" I ordered, hurting his sense of loyalty, "don't get involved" I murmured as well, dismissing his help without any consideration, after all, he hadn't been very loyal in letting the fraud incite my furious calculations, she had gone so far that my fire was one crackling roar (it's easy to work out that two plus two makes four under the shade of a fig tree, but I'd like to see someone right in the fires of hell draw lines and segments, create a perfect circle, and even prove theorems), I only know that I collected myself and, determined, took another step forward, scorching her, saying "types like you drool for a boot, types like you drool for a foot," perfectly balancing the ambivalence of what I suspected—her will to power mixed with the sensuality of submission—but she was flexible, this little miss, throwing her shoulder bag inside the car she rested her hands on the car's bodywork as if asking me to hit her, and it was obvious

what she wanted, but I didn't really want to smack her "you
think I'm into hitting you, do you, idiot?" and seeing in this
perhaps a step backwards, a weakness, or who knows what,
and making her own associations, she sparked back, metal-
lic, and her scornful laugh cut me "ha ha hah … you faggot!"
was the sharp bite the piranha gave me, trying to castrate
me with a single swipe of her knife ("obviously! …"), yet,
like the carnival trannie, the thick hairs of her ideology gave
her away, she who trumpeted her protest against torture
while at the same time being a shameless torturer in daily
life, just like the people, made in her image there in the football stadiums,* just like the government, the oppressor, that
she fought tirelessly, I only know that's what stopped us in
our tracks, the circus caught fire (a mask lay on the ground
in the ring), my architecture collapsed in flames, including
its iron structure, and burning myself I said "whore," it was
an explosion in my mouth and my hand flying another explosion in her face, and the good smack in the face wasn't
part of a ritual, I now intentionally used the palm of my
hand together with the repressive weapons in her arsenal
(yes, I'd give her both an outburst and a beating!), so I said
"whore" again and again my hand flew out, and I saw her
rosy skin stain red and her whole face be covered suddenly
by a swarm of ants, tears welled up in her eyes, I watched
closely, my eyes burning into her face, she didn't move, sup-
ported herself on the car, I had steel in my backbone again,

she, savoring the lascivious recoil from the smack, skillfully crystallizing a complex system of gestures, her hair disheveled, enjoyed, almost to the point of orgasm, the sensual drama of her own position, but none of that surprised me, after all I knew her well, the caliber of the thrashing didn't matter, she had never had enough, just what would do, at that moment it was clear that I held the pendulum that had sure control over her movements, it was clear that I had decisively changed the way time went round, knowing, as I knew, the immense realms of her gluttony still left to explore, knowing, as I knew, what changes I was capable of, and it was right here in me that I thought "just wait, you'll see" "just wait, you'll see all right" was what I thought as I realized that the shit filling my mouth was already leaking out at the corners, but I didn't lose any of this intimate substance, I caught on my tongue whatever was about to drip, what's more the moment's billowing smoke was extremely favorable to occultism, and I wasn't going to waste this chance to practice the sorcerer's fine arts, so it was like this: combusting drops of fat appeared on the metal of my cheeks, my face started to change, first the surface of my eyes, and right afterwards the obscene mass of my mouth, in an instant I was the bastard I was in bed, and in the glow of her eyes I read "yes, bastard, you're the one I love," and always attentive to the signals of her flesh I started to use my tongue silently, sinuously it worked its way into the most inconceivable of positions, and it wasn't long before she moved her lips softly and said an ambiguous "you dirty man," you needed to know her mouth up close to get what she was saying, and you needed to know this girl and her various moods to get her suggestion, I pretended that I'd forgotten everything and that the world had been squeezed down to that one meter in diameter, I was still the bastard I was in bed and she said "you dirty man" again in a more salacious way, it was the same as saying "ask me to lie down on the lawn," she who in her bucolic raptures would always ask me to screw in the woods, so I formed a viper from the slimy muscle of my tongue, gave it a head and a mean arrogance, "m" "m" "m" I said, with a flick of its salacious tip, "dirty man, dirty man" she said with hypnotized abandon, perhaps already entering a state of grace, still keeping her nostrils flared, her noisy breath rippling over her body, her pert breasts rising and falling, all the feathers of her body at the ready, in this situation it made no difference if you said that the bird was prepared for flight or that the bird had spread its wings on the ground, and it was to make her even more drunk with desire that I lifted my hand close to her face, and began to run my middle finger along her lower lip, and first there was a trembling, then an intense burning, slowly her mouth was opening for a perfect performance, and we started to say things to each other through our eyes (this language that I also taught her), and attentive to her mouth, I got it to fake as if it were ... I was clearly saying with my eyes "you'd never imagined that your body had a spot so perfect for this finger of mine until I penetrated you and you moaned," and immediately her eyes screamed back at me "dirty man dirty man dirty man" as if they were saying "tear me open bleed me step on me," and I felt the tip of her tongue touching my finger, furtively licking my nail, and felt her teeth, that were no longer sharp, nibbling the humid pulp, she sucked greedily on my bait, we were watching each other, and birdlime oozed from her pupils, and it was just as if I were hearing what she'd said so often in that ambivalent way "I never met anyone who works like you, you're the best craftsman for my body, no question," and so I carried on modeling a wantonness in her mouth, and then my hand slid down to the plaster of Paris of her throat, and it didn't take long before her ravenous sucker-pores swallowed my fingers, and with my dirty mouth I said "I'm barefoot" and saw how a stark despair took control of her, but without rushing I said "I'm not wearing socks or shoes, as always my feet are clean and moist" and suddenly from her eyes I heard a crazed cry for help "loose all your demons on me now, it's only with them that I can come," and listening to this strangled moan I, the bastard, whispered "you remember the foot I once gave you?" and here she said "my

love" as if she were suffocating, and I, the old man, reminded her "it was a foot as slim and white as a lily, remember? ..." and slowly closing her eyes she said "my love my
love," and I, the bastard, even asked "what did you do with
the foot I once gave you? ..." and now in agonies she sighed
"my love my love my love" and that's when I saw I really had
my foot on her, and that—in my forge—I could turn the
supposed rigor of her logic upside down, because if I said
with a sigh "you see how many things I've taught you?" she
would have to say "yes my love yes" and if I also said "why
persist so much in trying to teach me?" she would have to
say "forget it my love forget it" and if I said to her "it's day
already, your common sense stretched its limbs long ago,
which path is it wandering down now?" she would have to
say "no idea my love no idea" and seeing the sacred and
obscene heat simmering in her flesh I would be able to say
"be more careful in your judgments, put some of this burning material into them too" and she would agree without
hesitation "of course my love of course" and remembering
the scorn which she had heaped on me, I still the bastard,
could get the last word, saying "and who is your only man,
the clay of your clay?" and she as loyal as ever would reply
"you my love you" and I'd even be able to put my tongue in
her earhole, until it reached the little uterus deep in her
skull, and spitting my blood in a well-aimed fiery gob, say
"the one who uses reason incorporates his passions into it,"

imbuing the gray hydrangea hidden there with a deep red, sending that anemic flower mad for good, making a new species germinate with my thick sperm, a new species that for all I cared could live or die, because in fact it was only to save a few moments that, notwithstanding my huge turmoil, I was rioting, she got on my nerves with her visits, getting in my way every day, but I didn't say or do any of this, and for a while I just continued to look at her numbed, crushed face beneath my feet, examining without any mercy, almost as a doctor would, the by-product of my sorcery (hadn't I told her a hundred times that pious prostration and the erection of a saint are mutually dependent?) as I listened to her anointed lips stripping in an obsessive delirium "my dirty love my dirty love my dirty love," and when I felt her little hand trembling as it slid under my shirt, become a finch that has flown from a nearby thicket to nest in my chest hairs, it was only then that I washed the bastard from my face and in a flash pounced, she was a white sheet of fear as I roared "take it! take the other one too!" and held out the foot like a soldier would "at least take the big toe and put it between your legs, since it so tickled your clit" I was shouting "go on, fucking bitch, it's the only thing I'm leaving you, cut off the big toe while you've got the chance" and I saw her dumbstruck face, the free and easy turtle, I'd known how to make her feel the weight and torture of a shell again, I'd reduced her reaction to an agony, I saw the terror in her eyes, it's not enough to sacrifice an animal, you need to send it off with the right ritual prayers too "snap out of it, not a bit of my body ever again, nothing! nothing! you'll go to the dogs too!" I was also shouting, knowing that I was digging a deep pit in her memory forever "nothing! nothing of my body ever again" "you're not human" she said coming out of her daze "you're not human" "out! out! you'll go to the dogs too!" "you're not human, you're a monster!" "get out, get out of my life once and for all!" "you're a monster, you scare me" "so fuck off, fraud" "I'm scared" "fuck off" "scared scared" "fuck off fuck off" I screamed almost happily, as her car slithered crazily in reverse, not finding the way out, although the gate was open, I hadn't even noticed, and sticking her head out she was still shouting "you're not human" and I was there pushing her car further out of control, kicking her out with a mixture of anger and laughter "fuck you, you little closet fascist" "your mother's a fat sow," "your mother loves dick" "you degenerate cum" "you piece of short-billed pipit shit" all of that ladled out with true pleasure, not to mention that Bingo was backing me up fully in the brawl, barking like he never had, carrying out dangerous leaps and spins, even throwing himself at the wheels, and then there came a terrible "limp dick!" that she shouted from the road before hunkering down behind the steering wheel with the usual extras: the wet, red cheeks and the big, generous tears rolling down them, and the girl that she was, just like most of them, she wanted me as her son, but (being emancipated) wanted me much more as her man, I only know that to drown out the fury of her car accelerating away I almost tore my mouth with a "fuck you" and no longer seeing Antônio's legs, but only the bush rustling, I gathered my strength and bellowed a "fuck the whole world!," ripping my chest open, bursting my jugular, having a grand old time with my scandalous behavior, noticing a demure window on the hillside opposite open and close with a single gust of wind, but I screamed "fuck you all! fuck you all! fuck you all!" and with this was bringing up offal, pluck and tripe, I was surprised and touched to see the other side of me, I even felt like turning somersaults on the lawn (only then realizing that I'd misjudged her size, she wasn't even a dwarf, she was an insect, an ant), but instead of abandoning myself to monkeying around gleefully, I stood there for a while, looking at the ground like a hanged man, my body tangled in the threads of this swindle, my innards shredded by the acid's action, an actor in the raw, in absolute solitude—without an audience, a stage or lights, under an already glorious and indifferent sun—struggling with a din of bloods and voices and with more distant gravel, and suddenly my thoughts drifted to her, and to the forlorn seclusion of her house at this breakfast hour, by now she'd certainly be sat looking to the side, that was what she always did after her frugal breakfast, one elbow propped on the table, her head cupped in her hand, her eyes fixed on the past, her advanced widowhood trickling by for hours on end, reliving day by day the old times of our unity, ruminating from early in the morning on the remains of the myth, having silently witnessed, year after year, the noisy destruction of all principles, and I also remembered the most intense page in her book of wisdom (next to the sermon against egoism), for even though her offspring had been scattered she was still the spiritual keeper of a rare heritage, the lesson that she always repeated on the rare occasions she saw me, a son only abandons his home when he takes a woman as his wife and raises another house in which to beget children, and his children more children, and this was nature's spontaneous course—procreation and providing for the family through work ("love is the only meaning in life"), and from that I passed straight to the old photo, mother and father sitting down, she's resting her hands in her lap and has a pious look in her eyes, one foot crossed behind the other, he looks solemn, his chest thrust out, a kernel of silver holds his collar closed without a tie, and then there's his angular face, befitting a tough farmhand, his thick moustache, his iron gaze, and the small crowd of their children standing around them, mineral, well-behaved, the odd mouth twisted in a rictus, an unsuccessful attempt to meet the photographer's frivolous demand, and there I lingered among the foundations and the supports and the

unshakable beams of our greenhouse, we had short legs
back then, but under that roof every step we took was safe,
the soft hand that guided us seemed always to be lucid, and
without a doubt there was something gratifying about the
solidity of the chain, the joined hands, the simply laid table,
the washed clothes, the measured words, the cut nails, everything within its limits, everything occurring in a circle of
light, in strict opposition—no patches of half-light—to the
dark place of sins, yes-yes, no-no, the stain of imprecision
was of the devil, it was in childhood (in mine), no doubt
about it, that the world of ideas was found, complete, perfect, undebatable ideas, which I now—in my turmoil—
barely glimpsed in memory (even though the reverse side
of each one was inscribed with "guilt improves man, guilt is
one of the world's driving forces"), while at the same time
I believed piously that words—impregnated with values—
each of them carried, yes, in its core, an original sin (just as
a passion is always concealed behind every gesture), it occurred to me that not even the tub of the Pacific would have
enough water to wash (and calm) such vocabulary, and
there, empty-handed in the middle of that devastation, with
nothing to lean on, not even a cliché, I only know that I
suddenly let myself drop like a load, I literally ended up
prostrate there in the courtyard, my head buried in my
hands, my eyes an itching swarm of ants, shaking all over
from a terrible explosion of sobbing (hoarse moans pulled

from deep inside), until my arms were lifted by heavy peasant's hands, Dona Mariana on the one side and Antônio on the other, he clumsy and silent, she casually at ease in spite of her bulk, straight away trying to distract me with what she was saying, cajoling me gently that I couldn't not pass by the hutches before "running off to São Paulo," saying she was "perplexed" with Quitéria's young, "the girl had thirteen in her first litter, thirteen! who'd have thought?" and reminding me that "Pituca sired them, that naughty old rabbit, still at it at his age," "perplexed!" repeated Dona Mariana in her lullaby, only altering her tone to give a half-whispered scolding to her husband, who wasn't pulling his weight, the two of them trying to lift me off the ground as if they were lifting a boy.

The Arrival

AND WHEN I arrived at his house, at kilometer 27 on the road from town, I was surprised the gate was still open, since the late afternoon had almost turned to night, whose atmosphere, I noticed getting out of the car, had gathered early in the bushes, the black, erect gravitas of the cypresses impressing me a little, and there at the foot of the stairs I also noticed that the door to the conservatory was wide open, which could be construed as another sign, redundant and almost too obvious in fact, that he was waiting for me, although the device was more likely there to remind me that I, even if late, would always go and see him, that I was unable to dispense with the rewards a visit would bring, and indeed I went pensively up to the landing, and stopped there for just a moment before going into the conservatory, where I saw myself watched by Bingo, an angry mongrel who fitted his role as the monastery dog perfectly, he was sitting rigidly immobile on a cushioned chair, the blade of his eyes slicing through the dull hour, but I ignored him, not only because I was used to him, but also because I'd spied the piece of paper on the table, on which I could read when I got closer, without picking it up, or even bending over, "I'm in the bedroom," typical of his messages—brief, a calculation stripped down to the bone, and even written in a forged schoolboy's scrawl—but then I immediately forgot the simulated casualness of the message and entered the living room, unhurriedly taking stock of what he'd left scattered across the floor, the two cushions that a little earlier would have served as his pillow, the wrought-iron lamp beside them, the thermos flask on the stool, an ashtray within arm's reach, and another reference work splayed open on the floor, with its spine facing upwards and clearly stating the contents of the tome, not to forget his beaten-up sandals of raw leather, carelessly discarded like those of a child, shards isolated from each other which I was reluctantly piecing together into a mosaic as I stood there for a moment, weighing the density of the quiet house, "my cell," according to the curt comment he had made one day, mixing in this stoicism both monastic and worldly things, until I moved through these fragments to the other side of the room and now I only had to cross the hall to reach his bedroom, which floated lazily in the calm light of a candle: lying on his side with his head almost touching his tucked-up knees, he slept, and it wasn't the first time that he had faked sleeping like a little boy, and nor would it be the first time that I would attend to his whims, because a virulent, vertiginous tenderness took hold of me, so sudden and un-expected that I could barely contain the impulse to open myself completely and prematurely to welcome back that enormous fetus.

Translator's notes

p. 29: An allusion to a Fernando Pessoa poem, well known in the Portuguese-speaking world and much translated into English. In Richard Zenith's translation *Autopsychography* (Penguin Classics), the referenced stanza reads:

> The poet is a faker
> Who's so good at his act
> He even fakes the pain
> Of pain he feels in fact.

p. 45: The section from "let cities fall" to "dying in the distance" quotes a poem Fernando Pessoa wrote as Ricardo Reis, an ode about chess players whose first-line title in Portuguese is *"Ouvi contar que outrora, quando a Pérsia."* The narrator of *A Cup of Rage* starts quoting in the seventh stanza of the poem, then jumps back to the start and end of the fifth stanza for the lines from "when the ivory king's in danger" to "dying in the distance."

68

In Nassar's Portuguese, the narrator quotes the poem word for word, except for the lack of initial capitals and line breaks, until he says "*nada pesa*" (it doesn't at all weigh on you) instead of the poem's "*pouca pesa*" (it hardly weighs on you), perhaps a natural alteration for a narrator who has none of Pessoa's understatement.

p. 50: A note by the author in the first published edition (1978) in Portuguese and reprinted in the new definite edition (2013, Companhia das Letras) mentions that the first published edition (1978) is a second version. The first was written in 1970 but not published. He mentions that the 1978 version expanded the chapter "The Explosion" and grafted on some lines by Jorge de Lima ("burn me, O Fiery Mouth ... transform me into your glowing embers ... sweet and violent fire," all from the poem "Espírito Paráclito," which could translate as "The Paraclete Spirit"), as well as allusions to Fernando Pessoa (mentioned in the note above) and James Joyce. The passage from "do you know what I think of you, compared to me?" to "when you do, you don't know it; that's the only difference between us, just that" is based loosely on a passage in James Joyce's *Portrait of the Artist as a Young Man*. The passage starts when Temple says to Cranly, "Do you know what I think about you now as compared with myself?"

p. 52: Brazilian football crowds shout "bicha," i.e. "faggot," at referees they don't like.